BAREFOOT BEAR
AND THE
ICE CREAM FACTORY

ISBN 0-8300-0340-1

Barefoot Bear and the Ice Cream Factory
was prepared and produced
by Tern Enterprises, Inc.
Sagaponack Road
Bridgehampton, New York 11932

Color separations
by Hong Kong Scanner Craft Company Ltd.

Printed and bound in Hong Kong
by Leefung-Asco Printers Ltd.

Barefoot Bear™ is a trademark of
Tern Enterprises, Inc., Bridgehampton, New York

Produced exclusively for **Kaleidoscope**

BAREFOOT BEAR
AND THE
ICE CREAM FACTORY

by Cindy West
Illustrated by June Goldsborough

KALEIDOSCOPE

Barefoot Bear loved to ride his bicycle. He loved to pedal as fast as he could around and around the block. One day, Barefoot rode off to visit his friend Natalie.

Barefoot pedaled so fast, he was almost out of breath when he got there. Natalie was in the backyard, feeding her kitten, Mittens.

Barefoot got off his bike and walked over to her. "Come out and ride with me!" said Barefoot.

"Where are you going?" Natalie asked.

"Down the street. If you come with me, we'll probably have a terrific adventure!"

"Sure," Natalie said. "But I want to take Mittens with us."

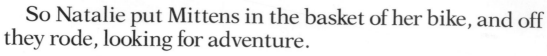

So Natalie put Mittens in the basket of her bike, and off they rode, looking for adventure.

"Whew! It's hot!" moaned Natalie after they had gone a few blocks. "It sure is," sighed Barefoot.

Natalie's eyes grew larger as they rode past Happy Harry's Ice Cream store.

"Hey!" said Barefoot. "I have some money left over from my birthday. I can treat us both to ice-cream cones!"

"I'd like a Rocky Road, please," Barefoot said. "And I'd like a Strawberry," decided Natalie. They sat on a bench and licked their cones.

Suddenly they heard a loud, screeching sound:
"Waaaaaa-ooooooo! Waaaaaaa-oooooooh!"

Sure enough, a few seconds later, two fire trucks sped by wailing their sirens. Barefoot leaped up from his bench.

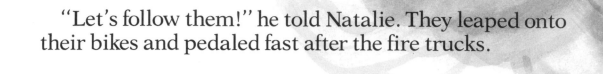

"Let's follow them!" he told Natalie. They leaped onto their bikes and pedaled fast after the fire trucks.

"I think they're stopping at the end of the block," Natalie called. She pointed at a big building that had smoke and flames coming out of it.

"It's a huge fire!" shouted Barefoot. He stared and stared at the flames until his eyes became dreamy, and closed.

When he opened them, Barefoot found himself riding on the back of the fire truck! He wore a shiny slicker and a big fire helmet and very big black rubber boots!

"Get that hose off the truck—*fast!*" ordered the fire chief. "The ice-cream factory's on fire!"
"Yes, sir!" answered Barefoot.

Barefoot and the other firemen unrolled the huge hose and passed it along to the chief. The chief attached the hose to the fire hydrant and turned it on.

"*Whoooooosh!*" A big blast of water shot out of the hose. The firemen put a ladder up against the building and climbed up with the hose.

"Stay back!" Barefoot warned the crowd that gathered to watch. "This is a dangerous fire! I hope they put it out before the ice cream melts!"

Suddenly, Barefoot was hit by a big splash of water. "Hey" he yelled. "Watch where you're aiming that hose!"

The fire chief raced over to Barefoot. "The hose is leaking!" he groaned. "See?"

Barefoot looked down at his feet and saw a hole right in the center of the hose. So much water was leaking out that there was no water left to fight the fire.

"Quick!" yelled the fire chief. "Get something to plug up that hose!"

Barefoot rushed to his right and rushed to his left, but
he didn't see anything to plug the hole with.

"Ouch!" he yelled, as he tripped over the hose and fell down. Barefoot rubbed his eyes and looked around him. All he could see were his big black rubber boots.

"Hey!" he said. "I bet I could plug up that hole with my boot!" Barefoot tugged off his right boot. Then he pushed and squeezed it into the hole in the hose.

The water stopped coming out of the hole—and shot
out the front of the hose just the way it should!

"Good work!" praised the fire chief. "I think we'll have this fire under control very soon!" Barefoot beamed as he watched the firemen put out the fire.

Barefoot stood up so quickly, he forgot he was wearing only one boot.

"Oof!" he cried as he fell back down, down, down, down, and closed his eyes . . . .

When he opened them, Barefoot found himself lying on his back on the grass. His bicycle was lying next to him.

"What happened?" Barefoot asked.

Natalie came over and sat down next to Barefoot. "Your bike hit a rock in the sidewalk and you fell off."

"Oh." Barefoot looked around. His bicycle was lying in the grass, and next to it was his very squashed Rocky Road ice-cream cone.

"What an awful adventure!" moaned Barefoot. "I hurt myself, and I lost my ice cream, too!"

"I lost my kitten," moaned Natalie. "The fire sirens scared her away. I've been calling and calling, but I can't find her."

Barefoot jumped up quickly. "I'll find her!" he promised. Barefoot looked and looked for the kitten, calling, "Mittens! Mittens!"

"Mew!" answered a tiny voice. "There she is!" Barefoot pointed to a branch of a big tree.

"Oh, Mittens!" yelled Natalie. "I'm so glad Barefoot found you. Please come down!" *"Mew!"* whined Mittens. She was too scared to move.

"Hmmm," thought Barefoot. If I were a kitten, what would make me come down?" Barefoot looked all around. But all he saw was his squashed ice-cream cone.

"Hmmm!" said Barefoot. He dipped his paw into the soft ice cream. Then he walked over to Mittens. Holding out his paw, he whispered, "Come get some ice cream, Mittens! It's really good!"

"*Mew!*" cried Mittens. She took a few steps down the trunk of the tree.

"Come closer," whispered Barefoot. Mittens took a few more steps, and then, suddenly, she raced down the trunk, straight into Barefoot's arms!

"Mew!" she called, licking the ice cream off his paw.

Gently, Barefoot handed Mittens to Natalie.
"Oh, Mittens, you're safe!" Natalie hugged her kitten
and smiled happily. "You saved my kitten!" Natalie told
Barefoot. "You're a hero!"

"I *am?*" Barefoot smiled shyly.

"Come back to my house, and we'll tell my mother all about our adventure."

When Natalie's mother heard the story, she told Barefoot she was very proud of him.

"I think you deserve a reward," she said. "How would you like another ice cream cone?"

"I'd love it!" shouted Barefoot. "But this time I'm not getting Rocky Road. I'll ask for good old Chocolate!"

Natalie and her mother giggled as they all walked home from the ice cream store.

"*Mew!*" said Mittens, who got one little taste of Barefoot's cool double-dipped chocolate cone!